American edition published in 2016 by Andersen Press USA, an imprint of Andersen Press Ltd.

www.andersenpressusa.com

First published in Great Britain in 2016 by Andersen Press Ltd.,

20 Vauxhall Bridge Road, London SW1V 2SA.

Copyright © Michael Foreman, 2016.

Distributed in the United States and Canada by Lerner Publishing Group, Inc. 241 First Avenue North, Minneapolis, MN 55401 USA

For reading levels and more information, look up this title at www.lernerbooks.com.

Color separated in Switzerland by Photolitho AG, Zürich. Printed and bound in Malaysia by Tien Wah Press.

Library of Congress Cataloging-in-Publication Data Available.

ISBN: 978-1-5124-0425-8, eBook ISBN: 978-1-5124-0448-7

1-TWP-7/1/15

TUFTY

The Little Lost Duck who Found Love

Michael Foreman

ANDERSEN PRESS USA

A family of ducks lived on an island in the middle of a lake.
At the edge of the lake there was a beautiful palace and a park.
Each morning the ducklings paddled along behind their mother.
The youngest, Tufty, always struggled to keep up.

"The Royal Duck and Duckess are very kind," Mother Duck told her children. "They always give us breakfast. See how they walk like us with their wings folded behind them."

Some evenings, Tufty and the other ducks
watched the Duck and Duckess dance at
grand parties under great crystal chandeliers.

As the golden summer passed, the nights grew colder and the ducklings cuddled closer.

"Soon, we will have to fly south where the winter is warmer," said Father Duck. "So practice your flying, little ducks."

One day, Father Duck said, "Time to go!" And off they flew,
up and away from the lake, and the palace and park.

Tufty was amazed to see that all around the park was a huge city. Roads and railways criss-crossed between towering buildings that seemed to touch the cloudy sky.

Poor Tufty struggled to keep up with the other ducks. The tall buildings made it even more difficult and soon he lost sight of his family.

He flew on, growing more tired and lost. Then it began to rain and get dark. "I must find a safe place to rest," he thought. Suddenly he saw what looked like an island amongst the traffic.

Tufty landed safely, but the noise of the roaring traffic all around was frightening. Exhausted, he took shelter in a tunnel leading down under the island.

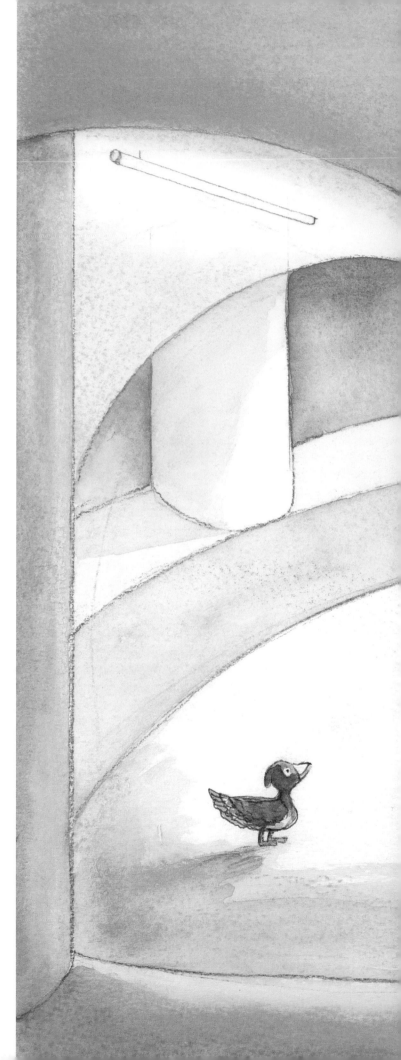

A man was sitting in the quiet tunnel.
"Hello, little one," he said. "This isn't a good
place for a duck. Here, have something to eat,
then we will find a better place for you."

The man shared his food with Tufty
and then scooped him up into his
arms. "Let's go, little one."

They left the
thundering traffic
behind them and came
to a dark wood next to a
small lake. The man moved
some branches from the foot of
a chestnut tree. "Welcome to my
home, little one," he said.

Tufty saw that the tree was
hollow, and inside was dry
with a bed of straw.
Feeling tired but safe, he
fell asleep in the man's hat.

In the springtime, as the days grew warmer, Tufty saw
flocks of ducks flying overhead. His family was returning
to the lake beside the palace. Tufty flew up to join them.

Together they flew back to the palace gardens.
Each day, more and more ducks arrived at the lake.

Tufty noticed a little brown duck. He thought
he had never seen anyone more beautiful.
"Let's get away from the crowd," he said to her
one day. "Let's spread our wings and fly away."

Together, they flew to the lake in the woods.
Trees were bursting into blossom and the chestnut
tree was more beautiful than any chandelier.

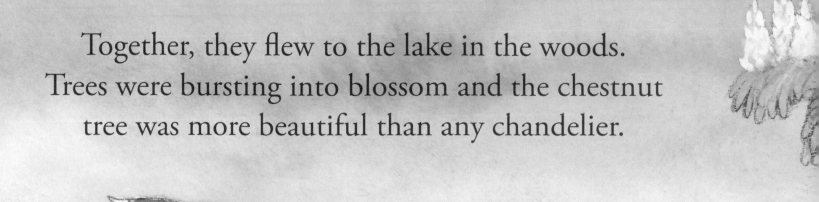

"Just in time for tea," smiled the man.
"Welcome home."